D1505652

CALGARY PUBLIC LIBRARY

JUL 2015

For my daughters, whom I cherish.
Proof that cuteness knows no age. – M. P. B.

For my daughter Molly, my love forever. – S. M.

tiger tales
5 River Road, Suite 128, Wilton, CT 06897
Published in the United States 2015
Text copyright © 2015 Margaret Park Bridges
Illustrations copyright © 2015 Shelagh McNicholas
ISBN-13: 978-1-58925-132-8
ISBN-10: 1-58925-132-6
Printed in China
LTP/1800/0996/0914
All rights reserved
10 9 8 7 6 5 4 3 2 1

For more insight and activities,
visit us at www.tigertalesbooks.com

I Love You Forever

by Margaret Park Bridges   Illustrated by Shelagh McNicholas

tiger tales

Mommy, what age
was I cutest of all?
Now that I'm bigger
or when I was small?

When you were born,
you were cuter
than cute,
Tiny and sweet
in your new
birthday suit.

Then you grew older
but cute as a pup,

Falling each time that
you stood or sat up.

Bold and determined, you loved saying "No!"

And going wherever I said not to go.

Next, you were giggly
and silly and fun,
Eager to climb . . .
and to jump . . .
and to run!

You were still cute
when you learned
to pretend,
Making up games
with your teddy
bear friend.

Clever and curious,
you wondered why:
"Why is there thunder?"
and "Why can't I fly?"

Kind to your friends, now you're helpful and fair,

Waiting your turn and delighted to share.

Watching you learning and growing each day,

I'm prouder of you than I ever can say.

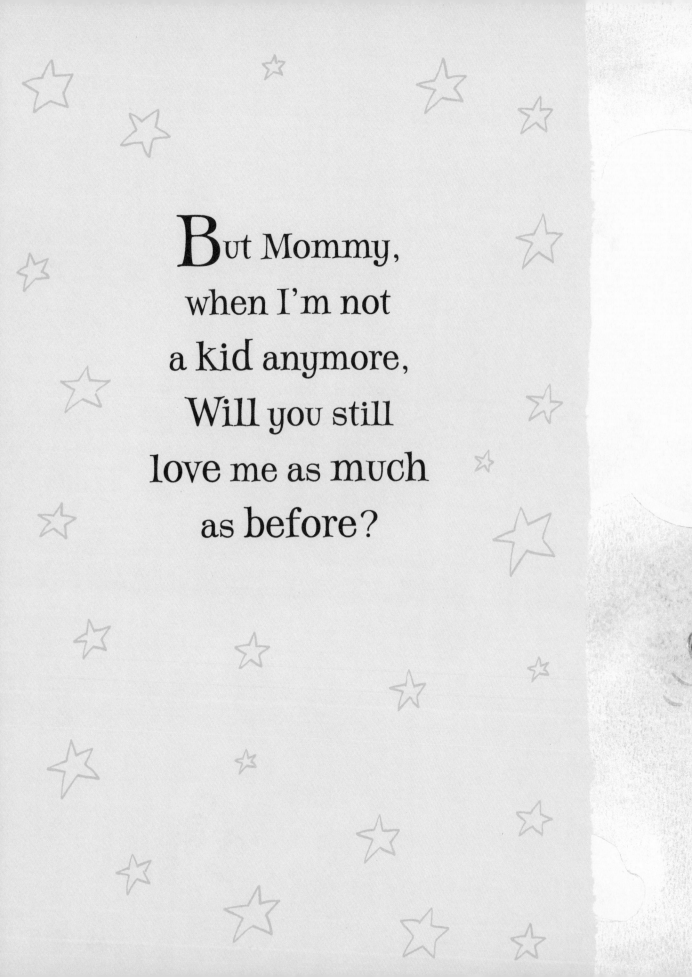

But Mommy,
when I'm not
a kid anymore,
Will you still
love me as much
as before?

Of course!
You're my **darling**,
no matter what stage.

I'll love
you forever,

whatever your age!